Airy Fairy

Magic Muddle!

Look out for more stories...

Magic Mischief!

Magic Mess!

Airy Fairy
Magic Muddle!

Margaret Ryan
illustrated by Teresa Murfin

SCHOLASTIC

For Lucy Charlotte,
with love

Scholastic Children's Books,
Commonwealth House, 1–19 New Oxford Street,
London, WC1A 1NU, UK
a division of Scholastic Ltd
London ~ New York ~ Toronto ~ Sydney ~ Auckland
Mexico City ~ New Delhi ~ Hong Kong

First published by Scholastic Ltd, 2003
This edition published by Scholastic Ltd, 2004

Text copyright © Margaret Ryan, 2003
Illustrations copyright © Teresa Murfin, 2003

ISBN 0 439 95926 8

Printed and bound by AIT Nørhaven A/S, Denmark

2 4 6 8 10 9 7 5 3 1

Chapter One

It was the start of a new term at Fairy
Gropplethorpe's Academy for Good Fairies.
Airy Fairy sighed as she pulled on her pink
school frock and her pink fairy shoes.
She loved living at Fairy Gropplethorpe's
Academy with the other nine little orphan
fairies. She loved the Christmas holidays at
school, with all the party games and delicious
food, but now it was back to difficult lessons.

Airy Fairy trailed out of her bedroom and looked down over the bannister into the big school hall. All the decorations had been taken down, and the hall looked a bit bare.

"I wish we could have holidays all the time," she said to her best friends, Buttercup and Tingle. "I like holidays. I could get ten out of ten for holidays. I'm good at holidays."

"You're not much good at anything else," sneered Scary Fairy, coming downstairs behind Airy Fairy and poking her with her wand. "Bet you don't get anything right this term. Again."

"Just ignore her, Airy Fairy," said Buttercup and Tingle, "she's a pain."

But it was very difficult to ignore Scary Fairy. She was clever and sly. She was always picking on Airy Fairy, but Airy Fairy was always the one who got caught. Especially by Miss Stickler, their teacher. Scary Fairy was Miss Stickler's niece and Miss Stickler thought she could do nothing wrong. She also

y Fairy could do nothing right.

airy sighed again. What a pity the

days had to end.

Airy Fairy and her friends took their seats at the front of the hall and waited for assembly to begin. As usual Scary Fairy slid in behind them. They stood up when Fairy Gropplethorpe came in, but she waved them all to sit down again.

"Good morning, Fairies," she smiled. "I'm pleased to see you all looking so bright and cheerful this morning. I expect you're eager to get back to your school work."

Not really, thought Airy Fairy, *I never seem to get any of it right. But perhaps things will be better this term. Perhaps over the holidays I'll have magically become really clever.*

She gazed out of the window and put on what she thought was a really clever expression. She screwed up her eyes and peered down her nose, but all that did was make her sneeze.

But maybe this term I will be top of the class, she thought, *and Miss Stickler and Fairy Gropplethorpe will be really pleased with me.* She could just picture herself going up on to the platform to receive a prize at the end of term for being the best fairy in the school.

It would be a really nice prize too, like an enormous box of chocolates or a picnic basket. Then she and her friends could slip down to the hall and have a midnight feast. She was just thinking about what might be in the picnic basket – cream buns, chocolate cake, fizzy pop ... when someone poked her from behind.

"Pay attention to Fairy Gropplethorpe," a voice whispered.

"Stop poking me, Scary Fairy," muttered Airy Fairy, and she reached behind her to poke Scary Fairy with her own wand.

"Airy Fairy, what ARE you doing?" said a stern voice.

"Oh no," gasped Airy Fairy, as she slowly turned.

Scary Fairy was no longer behind her. Scary Fairy had moved. In her place sat Miss Stickler. Miss Stickler had poked her to make her pay attention and Airy Fairy had just poked her back.

"Erm er, sorry, Miss Stickler," said Airy Fairy. "I thought it was ... erm ... er ... I didn't know it was you."

Miss Stickler glared at Airy Fairy.

"Not a good start to the new term, Airy Fairy," she said. "Not a good start at all."

And it got worse.

Fairy Gropplethorpe had news for the fairies.

"I have just had a letter from Fairy Noralott, the chief inspector of schools. She is concerned about how fit we all are. She thinks that because we fairies fly everywhere we are not getting enough exercise to keep us healthy."

I don't fly everywhere, thought Airy Fairy. *My wings are usually much too wonky for me to fly anywhere.*

"So," went on Fairy Gropplethorpe. "Fairy Noralott has asked me to organize the Fairy Olympics. This will be a competition to see who is the fittest fairy in the school."

"A competition," muttered Airy Fairy to Buttercup and Tingle. "I don't like the sound of that. In a competition someone has to come last and it's sure to be me."

But Fairy Gropplethorpe hadn't finished.

"The Fairy Olympics will take place in a few weeks' time, so, I want you to concentrate on getting fit, Fairies. I want you to take lots more exercise. Spend more time in the gym, more time out of doors, and less time flying everywhere. Wings are to be folded back neatly and I want you to walk everywhere instead."

"Oh, that'll take ages," whispered
Buttercup and Tingle.

"And I've got a hole in my fairy shoes,"
sighed Airy Fairy. "Still, at least we're not
going to have extra spelling homework, or
flying backwards lessons. I still bump into
things flying forwards."

"One more thing," said
Fairy Gropplethorpe.

"Fairy Noralott will be handing out a special prize at the Fairy Olympics for the best fairy in the competition. I wonder who will win it. You will all try really hard, Fairies, won't you?"

"Oh yes, Fairy Gropplethorpe," chorused the fairies.

"Oh help," said Airy Fairy. "I'm sure to be hopeless. I'm sure to get things wrong. I don't know my left from my right or my up from my down. I'm sure to get in a muddle."

"Stop worrying, Airy Fairy," said Buttercup and Tingle. "You'll be fine."

"No, you won't," muttered Scary Fairy to herself. "I'll get the special prize. You'll get everything all wrong as usual. I'll see to that."

Chapter Two

The fitness programme began right away. Miss Stickler sent all the fairies to change into their PE kit, then led them all to the gym.

"Right, Fairies," she said. "We've no time to waste. We'll start off with an exercise to warm us up. I want you to run round the gym in a clockwise direction. Begin." And she blew her little silver whistle. *PEEEEP!*

"Oh, I can run round the gym," said Airy Fairy. "Anyone can do that. Perhaps this won't be so bad after all." And she led the way.

Then she noticed the laces on her pink fairy trainers were loose. *That could cause an accident,* she thought, and bent down to tie them. Nine fairies crashed into her and fell over in a heap. *HELP!*

They all unscrambled themselves and stood up and rubbed their bumps and bruises. Airy

Fairy emerged rather dazed from the bottom of the heap.

"What an idiot you are!" Scary Fairy scowled. "You can't even run round the gym without causing accidents!"

Miss Stickler raised her eyes heavenwards. "Do try to be careful, Airy Fairy," she said.

"Yes, Miss Stickler. Sorry, Miss Stickler," said Airy Fairy.

"Right, Fairies," went on Miss Stickler. "Hopping on one foot now. Start with the right foot. Begin." And she blew her little silver whistle.

PEEEEP!

Airy Fairy paid close attention and copied exactly what Miss Stickler did.

But she was standing opposite Miss Stickler.

"You're hopping on the wrong foot, Airy Fairy," said her teacher.

"No, I'm hopping on the right foot," said Airy Fairy.

The other fairies giggled. Airy Fairy was always so funny.

"Change to the left foot, Fairies," called Miss Stickler.

Airy Fairy got a bit muddled. *If my right foot's my wrong foot, will my left foot be my right foot?* she wondered.

"I know," she said. "I'll just hop from one

foot to the other. That way I'm bound to be right some of the time. Or left."

Miss Stickler shook her head when she saw her. "Do stop being an idiot, Airy Fairy," she said.

Airy Fairy sighed and blew out her cheeks. No matter how hard she tried she was always in trouble.

"Now, Fairies," Miss Stickler went on. "We'll move on to climbing up the ropes. Find a partner. One fairy at the bottom of the rope to keep it steady while the other climbs up. Begin."

Airy Fairy looked round for Buttercup or Tingle, but before she could partner them, Scary Fairy rushed over. "I'll be your partner, Airy Fairy," she said. "You go first."

Airy Fairy reluctantly agreed and looked at

the rope. It went a long way up to the
ceiling. It would be so much easier just to fly,
but Fairy Gropplethorpe had said wings had
to be neatly folded back. Airy Fairy glanced
back at her wings. They weren't
exactly neatly folded.
More like really
squashed, with
bits of sticking
plaster on them
from when
she'd caught
them in her
bedroom
door.

"Oh well." Airy Fairy caught hold of the end of the rope and began the long climb to the top. It was hard work and her face was as pink as her gym shorts when she got there. But it was worth it. There was a really good view from the window. Airy Fairy could see the branches of the oak tree which surrounded the school. It just looked like an abandoned tree house to human beings. Airy Fairy could also see a red squirrel. He had come out to warm himself in the winter sunshine, and was sitting on a branch nibbling a nut. The sunlight glinted through his red bushy tail, and his bright little eyes winked at Airy Fairy.

"Oh, he's lovely," she breathed. She was so busy admiring the squirrel she didn't see Scary Fairy give the rope a sharp tug.

"Help," cried Airy Fairy as she lost her grip. She grabbed for the rope but it slipped through her fingers.

Aaaaaaaargh.

Wheeee.

Whump. She landed on Miss Stickler's head, sending her crashing to the floor.

"Airy Fairy," yelled Miss Stickler, who had put her knee through her stocking and bent her whistle in the fall. "What DO you think you're doing?"

"Nothing. I mean, sorry, Miss Stickler," gasped Airy Fairy, her legs in the air and her wings more bent than ever. "I fell off. I mean the rope moved. I mean I saw the squirrel then... I mean... Sorry, Miss Stickler."

Scary Fairy hurried over.

"I was holding the rope perfectly still, Aunt Stickler," she lied. "Airy Fairy is just so careless. I do hope you haven't hurt your head. Lean on me and I'll help you back to the classroom."

"Thank you, Scary Fairy. You're very kind. I think we should all go back to the classroom before there are any more mishaps."

Buttercup and Tingle were sympathetic as
Airy Fairy trailed back to the classroom.
"Scary Fairy must have yanked the rope,"
they said.

"But Miss Stickler will never believe that,"
muttered Airy Fairy and looked on miserably
as Scary Fairy insisted on putting a bandage
on Miss Stickler's head.

She had just finished tying it when Fairy
Gropplethorpe came into the classroom.

"Well, how did the first fitness lesson go?" she beamed. Then she noticed Miss Stickler's head, and all the fairies' bumps and bruises. "Oh dear," she said. "How did that happen?"

"It was all Airy Fairy's fault," smirked Scary Fairy. "She was the cause of all the accidents."

Airy Fairy looked at her feet and scuffed the toes of her pink fairy trainers. She just knew these Fairy Olympics were going to be a complete disaster for her. Scary Fairy would make sure of that.

Chapter Three

But Fairy Gropplethorpe was determined that the fairies should get fit.

"Change back into your school frocks, Fairies," she beamed, "and come outside. I have magicked up a little surprise for you."

The fairies and Miss Stickler trooped outside and sat among the branches of the oak tree. Fairy Gropplethorpe chose a stout branch and balanced on it. It creaked loudly.

"Today," she said, "we are going down into the garden."

"Shall we fly down, Fairy Gropplethorpe?" asked Airy Fairy, leaning over to peer at the ground below. *Oops*, she leaned forward too far and fell off her branch. Tingle had to grab her by the back of her frock till she swung herself up again.

"No," said Fairy Gropplethorpe. "Wings must stay neatly folded back. We're going to climb down. The surprise is waiting for us at the bottom."

"Climb down?" gasped Airy Fairy, taking another nervous peek. The ground was a long way away.

"Yes," said Fairy Gropplethorpe. "I have magicked up a little ladder. Look."

She pointed to the side of the tree and
there, snaking its way down to the ground,
was a little rope ladder.

"Help," cried Airy Fairy. "I'll never get
down that. I'm sure to trip over my feet or my
shoelaces. I'm sure to fall off."

"Oh no, you won't," said Buttercup and
Tingle.

"Oh yes, you will," muttered Scary Fairy.

"What's the surprise, Fairy
Gropplethorpe?" asked Buttercup.

"You'll find
out when
we reach
the ground,"
smiled the
head teacher.
"Now I'll lead
the way. Climb
down behind
me, Fairies,
one by one."

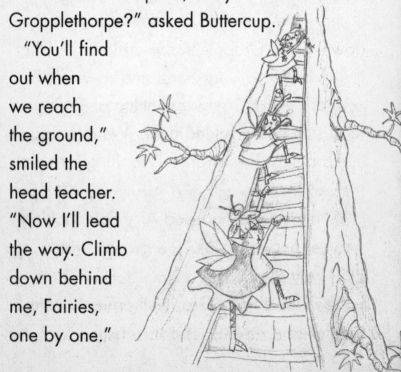

"You go before me," said Airy Fairy to all the other fairies. She waited until they were all safely down.

"Your turn now, Airy Fairy," said Miss Stickler. "Off you go."

Airy Fairy checked that her laces were tied and put her tiny pink trainer – her right one, or it may have been her left – on to the little rope ladder and began the long climb down. She was halfway there and was doing quite well, till she stopped to look down. Fairy Gropplethorpe and all the other fairies were on the ground and so was something else. A team of lively ponies. Fairy Gropplethorpe had magicked them up for a riding lesson.

"Oh, how lovely," said Airy Fairy. "I hope I get that little white one."

And she was so busy admiring it, she didn't see Scary Fairy at the bottom of the ladder give it a hefty push. It swung wildly from side to side. So did Airy Fairy.

"Aaaaaargh!" She tried to hang on, but she scraped her knees, her knuckles and her nose on the bark of the tree, and she let go and fell off. She went tumbling head over heels towards the ground and landed on the back of the little white pony. Facing his tail!

He got such a fright, he picked up his hooves and took off through the bushes. Airy Fairy hung on to him.

"Help, help!" she yelled. "I can't find the pony's head. Where did it go? It must be here somewhere!"

SWISH! The little white pony flicked his tail and nearly knocked her off.

Fairy Gropplethorpe and the other fairies
mounted their ponies and set off in hot pursuit.
They chased Airy Fairy past the bed of
winter pansies, past the rhododendron bushes
and over the crisp grass, still white and
sparkling from the night frost. They could see
Airy Fairy had her eyes closed. They could
see she was hanging on to the saddle for all
she was worth. They could see the garden
pond. So could the little white pony.

He gave a pleased little whinny and
stopped abruptly for a drink. *WHEEEEE!* Airy
Fairy lost her hold and sailed through the air.

WHIZZZZZ! She skated on her bottom across
the frozen pond ...

... till *SPLASH!* She landed in the icy water in the middle. *Cough, choke, splutter!* She spat out the pond water, swam to the edge of the ice, then hauled herself out.

When Fairy Gropplethorpe and the other fairies arrived she was standing at the side of the pond, sopping wet, and covered in slimy green weed.

"Oh, Airy Fairy, are you all right?" said
Fairy Gropplethorpe, taking off her cloak
and wrapping it round her. "You'll never get
to be a fit fairy at this rate."

"Huh, just look at her. She's not fit to be a
fairy," sneered Scary Fairy. "She should be a
warty toad instead."

Fairy Gropplethorpe helped Airy Fairy
back up on to the little white pony. "It helps if
you face the right way, Airy Fairy," she said,
and she took the reins and led Airy Fairy
safely back to school.

Airy Fairy climbed the long ladder back up to the Academy and, when she had changed into some warm dry clothes, went to join Miss Stickler in the classroom.

Miss Stickler had stayed behind to mark the spelling books. She had just reached Airy Fairy's when she arrived.

"Still nothing out of ten for spelling, Airy Fairy," she frowned. "You had better do some more."

Airy Fairy gave a deep sigh and took up her pencil.

"Spell bough," said Miss Stickler.

Airy Fairy wrote down *b* and stopped. "Is that bough as in tree or bow as in dog?" she asked, and, just to be helpful, she did her dog impersonation. "Bow wow. Bow wow. Ruff ruff ruff."

Miss Stickler closed her eyes and shook her head.

"Bough as in tree," she said.

"Got it," said Airy Fairy and wrote it down. *Bowgh.*

Miss Stickler looked at the word. She didn't look pleased.

Airy Fairy chewed the end of her pencil. "I haven't got it right, have I?" she said. "Sometimes I get a bit muddled."

Chapter Four

To make matters worse, later that week, Fairy Gropplethorpe had another surprise in store for the fairies.

"I have booked you all a session at the local Elf Club," she announced.

"Oh," said Airy Fairy. "Won't we all develop muscles if we go there? I don't think I want to change my name to Muscles the fairy."

"Don't be so silly, Airy Fairy," said Miss Stickler. "The Elf Club is very exclusive. It's where all the fairy pop stars go to keep fit."

"Perhaps we'll see Freddy Sprite," said Scary Fairy. "He's my favourite pop star."

"Perhaps we will," said Fairy Gropplethorpe. "But we are going there as part of our get fit campaign. Put on your warm coats and hats, Fairies, and we'll set off. No need to take your wands, you won't be doing any magic today."

Airy Fairy put on her pink fairy coat and pulled on her pink fairy hat. It was too big for her and kept falling down over her eyes and ears, so she didn't see Scary Fairy slip her wand into her coat pocket, and she didn't hear her mutter to herself, "I could do some magic at the Elf Club and muddle up Airy Fairy even more."

"Now stay in a neat line," said Fairy Gropplethorpe, when they had all got safely down the ladder from the oak tree. "Miss Stickler will lead the way and I'll bring up the rear."

"It's a chilly day, Fairies," said Miss Stickler, "so we'll march briskly to warm us up. Follow me and do what I do. Left right, left right. Swing your arms, heads up straight. Left right, left right. Lift your feet, stretch your legs. Left right, left right... Airy Fairy, what ARE you doing?"

Airy Fairy was doing a little dance in the middle of the line.

"Sorry, Miss Stickler," she panted, "I'm just catching up with the others. My hat fell over my eyes when I held my head up straight, so I couldn't see where we were going or what we were doing. But I was swinging my legs and stretching my arms. Right left, right left. Just like you said... What was it you said again?"

The other fairies grinned. They just loved Airy Fairy. She always made them laugh.

But Scary Fairy didn't laugh.

"She's a complete idiot," she muttered. "Why does everyone laugh at her? Why does everyone like her?"

"Just put one foot in front of the other and try to get to the Elf Club in one piece, Airy Fairy," sighed Miss Stickler.

The band of tiny fairies trooped down the country road, crossed where it was safe, and came to a halt in front of the Elf Club. To human beings the Elf Club just looked like a large abandoned dog kennel, half hidden by some hawthorn bushes, but inside it was Ollie's gym. Ollie was an old friend of Fairy Gropplethorpe's.

"Hullo, Henrietta, Miss Stickler, Fairies," he said. "Welcome to the Elf Club. Of course, this 'ere club's not just for elves, but for all fairy folk who wants to get fit. And Fairy Gropplethorpe tells me that's what you want to do, right?"

Not really, thought Airy Fairy, looking round her at all the fitness machines. *These machines look dangerous.*

"Now all the machines are perfectly safe," said Ollie, as if reading Airy Fairy's mind. "I'll show you how they work."

"Bet you still get them in a muddle, Airy Fairy," smirked Scary Fairy, giving her a sly pinch.

"Take no notice of her," said Buttercup and Tingle and put their arms round Airy Fairy.

Ollie explained how everything worked and the fairies got started.

Buttercup had a go on the rowing machine.

"Row, row, row your boat gently down the stream," she sang, as she rowed away to nowhere.

"This is fun," she said to Airy Fairy. "Why don't you have a go?"

It looked safe enough, but Airy Fairy wasn't keen.

Tingle tried out one of the weights machine.

"Wait a minute," cried Airy Fairy. "Are you sure that's not too heavy?"

"Oh no, it's fun," puffed Tingle. "Why don't you have a go?"

It looked safe enough, but Airy Fairy wasn't keen.

Then Miss Stickler came over.

"Why are you standing about doing nothing, Airy Fairy?" she said. "Choose a machine and get on with it. You'll never get fit at this rate."

Airy Fairy looked around. Buttercup and Tingle had swapped places and all the rest of the fairies were scattered around the room. She couldn't see Scary Fairy, but she did spy an empty walking machine. The one opposite was occupied by someone wearing sunglasses and purple shorts. And he was walking, walking, walking...

"I'll try the walking machine," she said to Miss Stickler. "That looks safe enough."

Airy Fairy stepped on and Ollie came over and set the machine to a comfortable walking pace.

"You'll be fine with that," he smiled. "See you in a bit."

Airy Fairy walked and walked.

"This is all right," she said, "but I wish I was going somewhere."

She looked at the man opposite. He was listening to his headphones.

"That's a good idea," said Airy Fairy. "This is a bit boring."

But no sooner had she said that than her machine speeded up, and she had to walk very fast to keep up. She panted and puffed and her cheeks became hot and very red.

Then the machine speeded up again and again and Airy Fairy had to run faster and faster and faster.

"Help," she yelled, as her little legs windmilled and her hair flew out behind her. Then, just as she thought she could go on no longer, the machine went *BANG*, stopped suddenly and pitched her forward.

The man in the machine opposite caught her as *WHEEE* she shot through the air.

"Hey, slow down, little fairy," he said. "What happened to you? What happened to your machine? It's got smoke coming from it."

"I don't know," gasped Airy Fairy. "It just went faster and faster. My legs couldn't keep up."

"Well, let's take a look," said the man, and took her hand.

Ollie came running over with all the others.

"I don't understand it," he said, scratching his bald head. "That's never happened before, and I checked this machine myself."

"Well, this little fairy's tired out now," said the man, "so, she and I will go and have a glass of juice in the cafe, while you find out what went wrong. What's your name, by the way, little fairy? Mine's Freddy. Freddy Sprite." And he took off his sunglasses and held out his hand.

"The famous pop star," gasped Airy Fairy. "WOW! I'm Fairy Airy. I mean Airy Fairy. From Fairy Gropplethorpe's Academy for Good Fairies."

Freddy Sprite grinned. "Pleasure to meet you, Airy Fairy," he said. "Come and tell me all about your school. I was hopeless at school. I never got anything right."

"Me neither," grinned Airy Fairy, and they went off together chatting like old friends. All the other fairies clapped and cheered and talked excitedly about Airy Fairy meeting Freddy Sprite. All except one. Scary Fairy had a really horrible expression on her face as Airy Fairy passed by, and Airy Fairy could see, sticking out of the back of Scary Fairy's shorts, her little fairy wand.

"We were supposed to leave our wands behind," she muttered. Then she thought, *Oh no, I bet that machine didn't go bang by itself. I bet Scary Fairy's been up to her tricks again. And now that I'm chatting to her favourite pop star, she's going to be worse than ever.*

Chapter Five

At the next assembly, Fairy Gropplethorpe had an exciting announcement.

"Good news, Fairies," she beamed. "I had a phone call from Freddy Sprite this morning. He's very interested in keeping fit, and in our Fairy Olympics, so he's going to drop in on the day to cheer us on. Isn't that splendid?"

"Ooh yes," said the Fairies.

"Oh no," said Airy Fairy. "I'm sure to be last. I wish I hadn't told him about it now."

"Stop worrying and just try as hard as you can," said Tingle and Buttercup.

"You're right," said Airy Fairy. "I'll try really hard. Maybe I'll be all right."

"You haven't a hope," muttered Scary Fairy behind her. "You're always in a muddle." And she sneakily loosened the belt on Airy Fairy's school frock and tied it to the back of her chair.

Fairy Gropplethorpe finished her list of assembly announcements and the fairies stood up to go. Airy Fairy's chair came too. She swung it round and clunked two fairies on the knee before the chair pulled her over backwards, leaving her stranded with her pink fairy trainers in the air.

"What ARE you doing now, Airy Fairy?" asked Miss Stickler.

"Nothing, Miss Stickler," said Airy Fairy, struggling to untie her frock. "Sorry, Miss Stickler. I got a bit tangled up."

Miss Stickler shook her head and gathered all the fairies together in a corner of the hall.

"Today," she said, looking at her timetable, "we are going to do cross-country running. We are going to climb down into the garden and, starting at the holly bush, run round the rhododendron bed, past the rose garden to the finishing line at the cabbage patch on the far side."

"Run all that way," gasped Airy Fairy, "but it's metres and metres. I'm sure to get lost. I won't be back until tomorrow."

"Nonsense," said Miss Stickler. "All fairies to report back in time for lunch. Now go and get changed into your numbered running vests and shorts."

"I'll never be able to do this," said Airy Fairy later to Tingle and Buttercup as she closed her eyes to climb down the little rope ladder into the garden. "The garden's very overgrown. I'll never find my way back."

"Yes, you will," said Tingle. "Look, follow me. I'm number 8. Keep number 8 in front of you and you'll be fine."

"Good idea, Tingle," said Airy Fairy, cheering up.

"That is a good idea," muttered Scary Fairy, who'd been listening. "I know how I can muddle up Airy Fairy even more now."

All the fairies lined up by the holly bush.

"On your marks, get set, go!" said Miss Stickler.

Airy Fairy set off. She kept right behind Tingle, keeping the number 8 in sight.

They went down the long straight path that led from the holly bush to the rhododendron bed. That's when things got tricky. The rhododendrons had grown tall and fat over the years and creeping ivy had grown round their lower stems. It sent out snaky tendrils to trip up unwary fairies. Airy Fairy was so busy keeping her eye on Tingle that her ankles got snarled up in the ivy and she fell over and bumped her head on a rhododendron root.

"Ow," she said, and sat for a moment or two rubbing her head.

That gave Scary Fairy her chance. She picked up a muddy stone and changed the 3 on her back to an 8. Then she ran in front of Airy Fairy.

Airy Fairy looked up. "Oh good," she said. "I can still see the number 8," and she set off after Scary Fairy.

Scary Fairy smiled and led her off the path, deeper and deeper into the rhododendron jungle, and further away from the rose garden. It got darker and darker as the rhododendrons closed in overhead.

"Surely we must be getting near the rose garden by now," panted Airy Fairy, and called, "Tingle, Tingle, wait for me."

But Scary Fairy ran on, and hid behind a large leaf. She waited for Airy Fairy to go past, then she headed back to the rose garden.

Airy Fairy ran round in circles. A green
frog leapt out at her and gave her a fright.
A large beetle vroomed across her path
and nearly knocked her over, and a huge
crow picked her up in his beak thinking she
might be a worm.
He deposited her
in a muddy
puddle when
he discovered
she wasn't.

Airy Fairy ran on. It began to rain. Great
fat rain drops slid down shiny green leaves
on to her head. Soon she was cold and wet
and completely lost.

"Help," she called. "Help. Where is
everyone?"

There was no reply.

Airy Fairy didn't know which way to go.

"Left or right," she said. "Which way is the
rose garden?"

She had no idea.

"Perhaps if I climb up to the top of that tall rhododendron bush, I'll be able to see."

She climbed all the way up, slipping and sliding and grazing her knees. But, when she got to the top, all she could see were the other rhododendron bushes.

"Oh no," cried Airy Fairy. "How am I going to get out of here? I can't do any magic because I've no fairy wand, and I can't fly because my wings are wonky. Perhaps I'm going to be lost here for ever and ever."

Chapter Six

Airy Fairy climbed back down the
rhododendron bush and sat down on a
big stone to have a think. *CLUNK!* Something
hit her on the head.

"What was that?" she said, and picked it up.

It was a pine nut.

"Where did that come from?" she
wondered. "I don't see any pine trees."

She looked round and there, sitting high up in the rhododendron bush, was the red squirrel she'd seen earlier.

"Hullo, Mr Squirrel," she called. "Can you help me? I'm looking for the rose garden and I'm lost."

The red squirrel swung easily to the ground and crouched down to let Airy Fairy climb on his back. Then he set off. Airy Fairy clung on tight to his tufty ears. Sometimes they travelled over the ground. Sometimes through the air.

The red squirrel brought Airy Fairy out, not at the rose garden, but at the cabbage patch. Most of the other fairies were there already and cheered as Airy Fairy slid off his back at the finishing line.

"Oh, you are lucky, Airy Fairy," said Buttercup. "Imagine getting a ride on a red squirrel. He was lovely."

"But where did you get to, Airy Fairy?" asked Tingle. "I thought you were following me."

"I was," said Airy Fairy, and told them what had happened.

"How awful," said Buttercup. "You could have been lost for days."

"Or weeks," said Tingle.

They were just about to head back to school for lunch when Scary Fairy appeared.

She stopped short in surprise.

"How did you get here before me?" she asked Airy Fairy. "I thought you were…"

"Thought she was where, Scary Fairy?" asked Tingle.

"Nowhere," muttered Scary Fairy, and turned and ran back to school, but not before the friends had noticed how muddy the number on her back was.

"Almost as though she'd changed the number then tried to rub it out again," said Buttercup.

"You mean she led Airy Fairy into the rhododendron jungle," said Tingle.

Buttercup nodded.

"Oh no," said Airy Fairy. "As if these Fairy Olympics weren't bad enough, I've got Scary Fairy's rotten tricks to worry about as well."

Chapter Seven

The day of the Fairy Olympics arrived, and all the fairies were up early to greet their guests.

"Put on your best school frocks," Fairy Gropplethorpe had instructed the fairies, "and remember to smile nicely and be polite."

But Airy Fairy couldn't find her best school frock.

"I had it on over the holidays when we all went out to tea with Mr and Mrs Goblin and all the little Goblins, but I don't know where it went after that ... oh yes I do!"

And she dived under her bed and found it in among the apple cores and sweet wrappers. Her best frock was in a terrible state. One of the little goblins had covered it in jam when he'd sat on her knee.

"Oh well, perhaps no one will notice," said Airy Fairy. "It's only a little bit crumpled and sticky."

Chief Inspector Noralott arrived at the Academy first.

"Ah, Fairy Gropplethorpe," she said. "How nice to see you. Your fairies are looking very smart. Well, most of them," she added, spying Airy Fairy's sticky frock.

Airy Fairy tried to cover up the jam stain with her hand.

"Let me introduce you to the fairies, Chief Inspector Noralott," said Miss Stickler. "This is my niece, Scary Fairy. She's our best student. And this, I'm afraid, is Airy Fairy, who's not."

Suddenly there was a flapping noise overhead and a large sparrowhawk circled the oak tree. He went round and round in ever decreasing circles, fixing them all with his yellow eye, till a figure dropped neatly from his back, and made a perfect landing on a sturdy bough. Freddy Sprite had arrived. The sparrowhawk swooped away as Freddy waved his thanks.

"Morning all," he turned to grin at everyone. "I told you I would drop in on the Fairy Olympics. And I've brought an extra special prize with me. I think you'll like it, so good luck to all of you."

The fairies went to change into their track suits, then they all climbed down into the garden. The grown ups took their places inside the upturned orange box the fairies had made into a spectator stand and the Fairy Olympics began.

First there was the ten-metre sprint held right in front of the spectator stand. Airy Fairy checked that her laces were tied and took a big deep breath.

"Try not to be last. Try not to be last," she kept muttering to herself.

READY, STEADY, GO. Miss Stickler fired the starting pistol and the fairies were off down the long gravel path. Scary Fairy elbowed her way out in front. Airy Fairy ran as fast as she could. She couldn't let Fairy Gropplethorpe down in front of Chief Inspector Noralott.

But where were the rest of her class? She could only see Scary Fairy ahead of her. She glanced behind her. There they were. She must be second in the race. But could she catch up with Scary Fairy? Then she remembered how fast she had run at the Elf Club when Scary Fairy had tampered with the walking machine. *VROOM!* Her little legs speeded up, she passed Scary Fairy, and crossed the finishing line first.

Airy Fairy couldn't believe it.

Neither could Scary Fairy.

"Where did you come from, Airy Fairy?" she hissed. "Everyone knows I'm the fastest fairy in the school."

But Fairy Gropplethorpe was jumping up and down and clapping her hands. "Well done, Airy Fairy," she called. "Very well done indeed."

"Nice one, little fairy," grinned Freddy Sprite. "Magic!"

"Was that the sticky fairy who won?" asked Chief Inspector Noralott.

Next came the pony race.

"Oh help," said Airy Fairy. "I must remember to face the right way this time."

"Bet you fall off again," muttered Scary Fairy. "I'll see to that."

But Airy Fairy heard her this time. Then she remembered how Scary Fairy had tied the belt of her frock to her chair at assembly, and she reached down and tied the laces of her trainers to the stirrups.

"I won't fall off this time," she said.

And she didn't. Not even when Scary Fairy poked the little white pony with her wand and made him rear up and gallop

faster than ever. Airy Fairy stayed on and
passed the finishing line first.

Airy Fairy couldn't believe it.
Neither could Scary Fairy.
"I don't know how you're doing it, Airy
Fairy," she said. "But I'll beat you in the
obstacle race. You're hopeless at climbing
ropes. You always fall off."
Airy Fairy gulped. She knew that was true.

The obstacle race was set up in front of the spectator stand.

This race had been Chief Inspector Noralott's idea.

"It will tell me how fit your fairies really are," she told Fairy Gropplethorpe.

There was a large climbing frame with ropes to cross, brown sacks to crawl through and a paddling pool to swim over.

Fairy Gropplethorpe wasn't keen on the race.

"At least let me put warm water in the paddling pool," she'd said. "It is winter time."

But Chief Inspector Noralott wouldn't allow it. "A little cold water never hurt anyone," she said.

The fairies lined up. Miss Stickler fired the starting pistol and they were off.

To her surprise, Airy Fairy climbed up and down the ropes with ease. This was much easier than climbing to the top of a rhododendron bush. Then she swung across the climbing frame.

Just like swinging
from the branches
of the oak tree.

Crawling through the dark brown sack was
no problem compared to the dark
rhododendron jungle, and, when she got to
the paddling pool, some of it had turned to
ice. Airy Fairy smiled, jumped on to the ice
and whizzed across it. She plunged into the
icy water in the middle.

"At least there's no pondweed in here," she spluttered as she swam quickly to the other side and hauled herself out and across the finishing line. She was too busy emptying out her trainers to hear the cheering.

She was too busy trying to get her wet hair out of her eyes to see Fairy Gropplethorpe beckoning her towards the stand.

"Go and collect your prize, Airy Fairy," whispered Tingle. "You've won the Fairy Olympics."

"What?" Airy Fairy could hardly believe it. Neither could Scary Fairy.

"How did you do it?" she muttered. "I bet you cheated."

"No, I didn't." Airy Fairy grinned. "With all your nasty tricks, you helped me practise. Thank you, Scary Fairy."

Scary Fairy made a scary face as Airy Fairy went up on to the platform to receive her prize. "Very good, Airy Fairy," said Chief Inspector Noralott, presenting her with a silver trophy. "You're the fittest fairy and a credit to Fairy Gropplethorpe's Academy."

"Well done, Airy Fairy," smiled Fairy Gropplethorpe, and she took off her cloak and wrapped it round Airy Fairy.

"You didn't slow down at all, little fairy," smiled Freddy Sprite. "I bet you're the fastest fairy in the world. Hey, that could be the title of my next hit song. Now here's the special prize I said I would present to the winner. Two tickets to my next concert."

"Oh, thank you," said Airy Fairy. Then she stopped and thought. "But I'm sorry, I can't accept them."

"Why not? Don't you like my singing?" said Freddy Sprite.

"I love it," said Airy Fairy. "But I've got more than one friend and it wouldn't be fair to choose."

"I see," Freddy Sprite was thoughtful too. "You know, Fairy Gropplethorpe," he said. "I think you have a really nice little fairy here, but my concert is a sell-out and there are no more tickets, so how about if I come to the Academy one day soon and sing to all of you."

"Oh, that would be wonderful," beamed Fairy Gropplethorpe.

"Er … erm … can I come too?" asked Chief Inspector Noralott.

"Everyone can come," said Airy Fairy, and held up her little silver trophy for all to see.

The fairies cheered and Airy Fairy smiled happily. She really needn't have done all that worrying. The Fairy Olympics had turned out brilliantly after all.

Meet Airy Fairy.
Her wand is all wonky, her wings
are covered in sticking plaster
and her spells are always a muddle!
But she's the cutest fairy around!

Look out for the other books
in this series...

Margaret Ryan

Airy Fairy

Magic Mischief!

How can one little
fairy get into such
BIG trouble?

SCHOLASTIC

Margaret Ryan

Airy Fairy

Magic Mess!

How can one little
fairy get into such
BIG trouble?

SCHOLASTIC